AF610598

Rock-a-Bye BabyGirls:

Short and Sweet Stories

By
Zorro Daddy

Zorro Daddy Publications

Before you get started …

Role playing, in a real life sense or online, is *assuming identities which are different from those in our everyday lives.* Countless themes in role playing cater to sexual preference, power exchange, fantasy and many more. Some affect the individuals in a physical manner. Others affect their emotions. Some even go so deeply as to affect the heart, the mind and the soul completely. One such theme of role playing is **infantilism**.

This book is by a heterosexual male. So the roles of infantilism used in this story are from a straight point of view.

What I write is always journey and an exploration into the subject of infantilism, not an. It is not a book that gives in-depth explanation of infantilism. (I only give a brief overview here in the introduction.) This is simply a collection of my literature about the subject, and Every word you read is a piece of my heart.

So, what is Infantilism? The only definitions you will read in this book are here. Firstly:

Infantilism – retention of childish physical, mental or emotional qualities in adult life.

Infantilism is a form of age play where someone regresses into the behavior and personality of a baby or toddler. They choose to do this for a number of reasons, ranging from a need for release of tension to the desire to live without adult responsibility.

Whether infantilism is something that is shocking to you or not, you absolutely must understand one thing right away.

ABDL-minded people become enraged when a parallel is drawn between infantilism and pedophilia. Infantilism is role playing between consenting adults. Pedophilia is a hideous crime that involves minors. There is no parallel between the two. It is the theme of the role playing in infantilism that leads people to call it pedophilia. This theme includes a care giver and a care receiver: An adult who role plays as a parent, and an adult who role plays as a baby, but they are both adults.

In the writings of this book, those two roles are "Daddy" and "BabyGirl". There is a dominant figure and a submissive one, much like in BDSM (Bondage, Discipline, Sado-Masochism) roles. Infantilism eliminates the BDSM part of it.

Some adults have sexual interest in infantilism. Others have no sexual interest in it. This varies by the individual. Some choose to live infantilism as their lifestyle while others choose to role play it on occasion.

That being said, there are a few terms I would like to explain before you get started.

AB (Adult Baby): An adult that chooses to regress to a state of mind she had when she was an infant. She will often retain the personality, and mannerisms of an infant. She finds interest in infantile things like toys, pacifiers, bottles, baby clothing, etc. Some even return to wearing a diaper. She submits to being treated, regarded, spoken to, and cared for as if she were a baby. She assumes the role of a baby/toddler.

DL (Diaper Lover): An adult who wears a diaper, but has no role playing as an AB.

BabyGirl: An adult female. Just as in everyday life, this is a term of endearment for a girl, but within the role playing of infantilism, it means so much more. This is explained as you go through this book, but please understand she is an adult female.

If you aren't aware of what infantilism is, hopefully this book will give you incite.

Rock-a Bye BabyGirls

Short and Sweet Stories

Stories by Title and Page Number:

Picture This:

Picture this: A quiet evening in a dimly lit living room. Outside a gentle brisk wind howls through the trees, giving the air a brisk feeling. It is the perfect night to cuddle close together and share warmth.

A beautiful BabyGirl is curled up in my lap. She seems content for the moment in her light-colored baby "t", and of course, she's nestled in the softness of her diaper. Wrapped in a soft blanket, she shifts a little to better position her head on my chest.

I gaze down at her with all the love that my beating heart has to offer. She gazes up at me with precious puppy dog eyes. A sheepish, playful grin forms behind the pacifier that slightly parts her pink lips.

The mood is relaxing, and a movie plays quietly on the T.V. but all I'm watching are the stunning eyes on this girl in my arms. She yawns lightly and her eyelids begin to grow heavy. Soon, she is asleep.

I rock her gently, and kiss her tenderly on the forehead as she shifts again and places her head on the side of my neck. I brush the hair out of her eyes, and whisper the only thought that races through my mind at that moment…… "I love you, princess."

I picture this every day, BabyGirl. Do you?

What Dreams May Come

You've gotta love of it. You've gotta live for it. The sight of her sleeping, curled up in a ball with lightly twitching eyes make it clear that her mind is off in some dreamy place.

Kneeling beside the bed, you gently stroke her hair. She's beautiful. Wearing something soft and light, like a nightie, she shifts her position ever-so-slightly. She moves her hips to find new comfort and in doing so, makes her diaper crinkle a little.

She's precious. Her head turns to the side, revealing the pacifier that has fallen from her lips. Trying not to disturb her slumber, you pick up the pacifier and attempt to put it back in her mouth. At first, she twitches her nose and moves her mouth away, but eventually cracks open her delicate lips, accepting the pacifier and lightly sighing relief over its return. She sucks on it once or twice, and then enters back into deep sleep.

You lean forward and kiss her forehead gracefully. You trace her eyebrows with your finger. Lying before you is a peacefully sleeping, fully grown adult female. Her appearance is enchanting. Her figure from, her tiny, painted toenails to the ribbons holding her pigtails in place, is an eyeful of infantilism.

It is obvious that she is in a blissful state, where she wants to be, how she wants to be, with who she wants to be. She is feminine in her manners and movement and essence. She is infantile in her demeanor and facade and emotions. She loves, whole-heartedly, and without reserve. She responds to love and kindness and lives vicariously through a bond that she has with you, her caregiver, and the owner of the passion within her heart.

She places her innocence in your hands and leaves herself in your care. You nestle her timidness. You shield her from her fears. You make her world and everything within it simple and pleasant and wonderful and loving, just as she is. There is nothing too overwhelming for her so long as you are there to ease her and to make her feel loved.

So you stand to your feet, and take in the sight of her once more before covering her with her blanket. You revel in the attachment that you feel to her. You turn to leave the room, and as you turn back to take yet one more look at her before closing the door, you find her looking at you, with eyes open and a bright grin beaming from behind her pacifier. She winks at you and then closes her eyes again.

You smile as you close the door.

The Spaghetti Incident

It had been a wonderful weekend so far. Just a pleasant, relaxing time at home. It was now Saturday evening, and I had just finished the dishes from supper. I walked over to the entry-way to the living room, and there on the rug was my precious AB Girl. At the moment, she was totally occupied with the coloring book and crayons in front of her.

Completely unaware I was watching her, she colored a little, but it was more like scribbling. She wasn't "old enough" yet to learn to color between the lines. She didn't have to worry about that right now anyway. It was fun to color, and her coloring book was none other than a collection of Disney® Princesses.

She lied on her tummy with her knees bent and her feet crossed. Her hair was wet, and in pigtails. Wearing one of my t-shirts (which was so big on her it could've been a nightshirt for her) and a new diaper that I had just put on her a few minutes ago, she was fresh out of the bathtub.

She rolled from side-to-side, playfully, and then onto her back. We made eye contact, and I winked at her. A smile formed behind her pacifier, and lit up her face. She began laughing hysterically as her pacifier fell from her lips, but luckily, I had wised up a little. I had begun attaching every one of her pacifiers to a ribbon, and clipping that ribbon onto her shirt. That way she'd never lose it, and I'd be able to find it for her when she needed it next.

Her laughter increased, and she covered her face with her hands. I began to chuckle, too. We were both recalling the events of an hour ago that turned out to be quite hilarious:

At about 5 o'clock, I started making supper. She wanted spaghetti. So that's what we had. The noodles came to a boil and were ready. The spaghetti sauce was cooked and was now cooling down. (She doesn't like the sauce to be very hot. She says it burns her mouth.)

All afternoon, I had been trying to get clothes on her, but she didn't want any. Not even socks. Just her diaper. And that's how she was when I lifted her up into my arms and carried her over to her high chair. Gently placing her in it, I fastened the table in front of her. I turned around to get her a plate of spaghetti and she began bouncing up and down in the high chair. Her feet didn't touch the ground. So she just kicked them in the air. It was obvious that she was excited about the meal she was about to eat.

I placed the plate of spaghetti on the little tray in front of her. Her eyes grew big, and she plunged both her hands into the spaghetti. She began mixing the sauce and the noodles, and while she was distracted with that, I did manage to get a bib on her. I realized that it would make little difference by the end of this, but thought it might help.

For a short while, she was content with just mixing the contents of her plate with her hands. Occasionally, she would look up at me and smile, and then go right back to mixing her food. Finally she had it mixed exactly as she wanted it. The spaghetti sauce covered her hands and went halfway up her arms by this time. Her face was partially covered with the sauce to as she had taken a few licks of her fingers along the way. But she wasn't done making a mess of herself yet. There was more to come.

She lifted up the first finger-full of spaghetti to her mouth and took the end of the noodles in her lips. Quickly, she drew the entire length of the noodles in her mouth. The sauce spattered all over her face, and now up into her hair! She chewed and swallowed. Then after a petite little burp, she giggled.

This was the scene until she cleaned her plate completely. And by the end of it all, she had spaghetti sauce all through her hair, all over her face, up and down both of her arms, on her chest, on the front of her diaper, and on her thighs. She was laughing uncontrollably as I took the tray off her high chair and placed it in the sink. When I removed the bib from around her neck, there was a neat little area that it covered which was clean.

"I'm glad I remembered to put your bib on you," I said to her.

She smiled and laughed and threw her arms up in the air.

"Bath time!" she exclaimed.

"You'd better believe it, BabyGirl," I said as I lifted her into my arms, re-assuring that I would need a change of clothes.

Luckily, I had thought ahead and had drawn her bath water all ready. On the way back to the bathroom, I began undoing the tapes of her diaper. I walked into the bathroom, removed her diaper, and lowered her directly into the bathtub.

She was just as animated during her bath as when she ate. As bubbles and her bath toys floated all around her, she splashed her arms in and out of the water, enjoying every second of it.

And now, she lay on the rug of the living room, clean for the moment, and laughed her head off at how silly the whole ordeal was. She sat up and put her arms out while signaling me with her hands to pick her up. I knew where this was going right away.

This precious little AB Girl had spent the evening satisfying her infantile antics, but now she felt really "little" inside and wanted to be babied. I lifted her up, carried her over to the couch, scooped up her teddy bear and blanket off the couch, handed them to her, sat down, and cradled her in my arms and on my lap. Her thumb went into her mouth and her head rested sheepishly on my chest. I kissed her gently on the top of the head.

For a few minutes, I rocked her lightly in my arms. Then, she removed her thumb from her mouth, and looked up at me while smacking her lips. It was time for a bottle. I had one ready for her. Foreseeing what she would want next and preparing for it made all the difference in the world. I was developing a sixth sense.

She took the nipple into her mouth, closed her eyes, and would have drunk it empty, except she fell asleep in the middle. I removed the bottle from her lips and offered up her pacifier that she unconsciously took in its place.

And there she remained for the rest of the night, asleep in my arms, as innocent and as infantile as the day she was born.

Every Little Thing

From a Distance:

I see her figure leaning up against the door frame at the end of the hall; she is silhouetted with light from a window. Her legs are long and go all the way up to her hips. My button down shirt covers her body down to mid-thigh. The shirt is unbuttoned by choice.

Her long hair, curled at the moment, dangles down over her shoulders. Her head is lowered slightly, a sign that she knows I'm eyeing her up, and she intends to enjoy it. Her eyes seem to pierce the darkness of the hallway. Her lashes seem to bounce when she blinks. The smile forming on her face makes her cheeks rise up. She's beautiful.

I walk up to her slowly and:

She gazes up at me, and reaches her arms out to me for my embrace. Her head fits perfectly under my chin, and she nestles herself in my arms. Her hug tells me every little thing.

I can feel her heart beating. I touch the back of her neck, and feel the temperature of her skin rising. Running my hands up into her hair, I breathe in her scent. Her eyes look up at mine, and our lips meet. I can't put to words how much I love this girl.

She curls her long legs around my waist, and I lift her into my arms, carrying her downstairs. She knows where we are going. I place my hand on her bottom to hold her up. She looks up at me, and smiles.

Why? She's a DL Girl, and I am her Daddy.

I carry her downstairs. She and her diaper are in need of attention. I lay her on the blanket on the living room rug. She reluctantly lets go of me, and settles to the floor.

Without missing an opportunity to delight her with surprises, I hand her that stuffed animal she's had since her birth. And her pacifier goes in her mouth.

Her body eases as I unfasten her diaper. She rolls around on the blanket because she likes the make her diaper changes difficult. Finally, my hands become the "tickle monster" to her sides. She laughs and settles herself down long enough to find her legs in the air and my hand cleaning her.

Her legs and bottom lower back down onto the blanket and a new diaper which she never saw me lay out underneath her. I draw the diaper up between her legs and into place, fastening it just in time for her to leap up and pounce on me with a giddy laugh only a little girl could have for her Daddy.

Pinning me to the floor, she wiggles her nose up next to mine.

I sit up and with her in my lap; I bury my face in her stomach, and blow raspberries into as she struggles to not spit her pacifier out in laughter. Gently laying her back down on the blanket, I swaddle her in it, wrapping her up and then I lift her up in the blanket.

I place her on the couch. She sits up, and I say, “Don’t go anywhere.” A big smile comes across her face. She knows I’m about to surprise her with something. She lies back down and curls up in the fetal position, trying to wait patiently for what it is. She can hear me in the kitchen.

From behind the couch I hand her a bowl of ice cream…chocolate. She sits up and crosses her legs Indian-style, and begins to eat it. I sit down with my guitar and begin playing it for her. She crawls from the couch to the floor for a front row seat.

And while singing to her, I look down at her. She is lying on her tummy with her feet crossed in the air. The tiniest little bit of her diapered bottom sticks out past my blue button down shirt. And she’s still eating that bowl of ice cream.

I’m reminded of the day I first met. We met in public at an ice cream shop. Very casually, we talked, not about ABDL or diapers or Daddies, but just about ourselves and each other. Little did I know on that day, she was wearing a diaper? She did this to see how it would make her feel while talking with her. So ice cream is a very important part of our lives.

She gets up and goes into the kitchen, getting rid of the bowl in the sink. Without even looking, I know she will be coming back with a can of Coke and a bottle filled with apple juice. She returns with both. She is done with the guitar concert, and wants time on my lap.

It's become second nature for both of us. She lies on my lap, cracks open the coke with her red fingernails and hands it to me. With her other hand, she hands me the bottle while lowering her head a little. For a few minutes she likes to regress and be bottle fed. Not so much because of the bottle, but because it gives her an opportunity to gaze up at me.

She's not really interested in being an AB, but she's a DL at heart. There are moments when she likes to be babied. This is one of them.

I take her in my arms and my lap. She rests her head on my chest and parts her lips to take in the bottle. I slowly trace the contour of her face: her jaw line, her eyebrows and the bridge of her nose. She reaches up and runs her hands down my cheeks. In a few moments, her eyes will grow heavy.

She finishes the bottle, and I roll her up on top of me. She turns her head to the side as I gently pat her back. She burps, and drifts off to sleep. And there we lay for the rest of the afternoon.

I see her every day, in my mind, in my thoughts, and in my heart.

What Is She Thinking About Now?

What is She Thinking About Now?

It brings a smile to my face just thinking about it.

When she opens her eyes in the morning, squinting from the sunlight, she sees you. A smile comes across her face… Why?

Maybe it was because you were the first thing that she wanted to see. Maybe it's because you were in the dream she just woke up from. Or the sight of you made her happy.

When you hold her in your arms, across your lap, she gazes up at you with a look of concentration on her face. She's not looking at your eyes. Instead, she traces your face, your eyes, your cheeks, your lips with her fingers. She sticks her finger in your hair and twirls it. And the touch of her fingertips to your face is so gentle and so caressing, you may wonder why she's doing it.

Perhaps she is affected by touch. And what your face feels like is a question in her mind. So the look of concentration on her face is *wanting to know*. So she decides to find out.

So you sit there holding her for a minute as she feels the morning scruff on your chin, and then you lean in and rub noses with her. She wriggles up her while laughing and tossing her head back and forth to avoid your "butterflies". As she does this, you peck her, ever so lightly, on the neck. She scrunches up her shoulders to try to stop the kisses, still laughing at what you're doing. It's obvious why she's doing all of that. It tickles, but she's not really trying to stop you. It's intimate attention, and a lot of fun, even if she's a BabyGirl who is ticklish on practically 90 percent of her body.

And now she lays back into your arms. You remove her pacifier and insert a bottle of milk. Instantaneously, she goes from giddy to calm. As she rests her head on your chest, now her eyes look up at you with a "grin" to them. She clutches the teddy bear in her arms tightly. She never stops smiling at you until the milk begins to take its effect on her. She nestles her face closer to your chest, and closes her eyes. How comfortable she must be. But what is she thinking about now?

Maybe she feels so safe and protected in your arms that she can drift off to sleep because she knows you will take care of her, and you will keep her safe. Or it could be that she's just simply tired. Either way, it's a sweet sight to see her curl up in your lap and fall asleep. It makes you feel so loved that you would almost shed a tear if a typical male impulse to not cry didn't take over and force you to stop.

And that moment, the very instant that she falls asleep, you see her face relax. If you have taken time to study her face and to study how she moves and reacts, you will know exactly what to do at that second. If she likes to sprawl out to get comfortable to sleep, she will do it subconsciously when she drifts off. If she likes to fall asleep on her tummy, she will want to do that, and if you are prepared to give her that comfort without losing her "pillow and mattress" (which is YOU!), you will be able to gently lay yourself down on the couch while never disturbing her and never moving her off your chest. It's a challenge of sorts, but one that every guy longs to take up.

When everything is so quiet, and she is very peacefully asleep, now the little things will begin to make an even bigger impact:

- *Routinely brushing the bangs (that keep falling down on her face) back up out of her eyes.

- Keeping a hand on her back, and an eye on the teddy bear, the pacifier.

- Knowing the position of her legs, especially if they're bent (so you don't get accidentally knee-d in the crotch.)

- The necessity the run your finger through her hair and kiss her on the forehead; a delicate reminder that you are still there.

Perhaps, ultimately:

- Recognizing that she really needs to sleep in a bed.

So you position one hand on her diapered bottom and the other still on her back, and you slowly sit up and stand up. All the while, you never disturb her. You carry her back to the nursery. And throughout all of this you don't wonder what she's thinking about. You wonder what she's dreaming about.

You place her in her crib amongst a "sea" of soft blankets and stuffed animals and whatever else she likes to sleep with. You take pleasure in knowing that she is still so quiet and serene because she feels safe. You gently lay her on her tummy and she *stirs to* for a moment, but it's okay because you have the "teddy bear and pacifier" trick to fall back on. She opens her eyes, and you reinsert the pacifier in her lips at the same time that you press the teddy bear against her shoulder. She takes the pacifier in her mouth and hugs the teddy bear, and just like that, she falls asleep again. You cover her with a blanket, and now she is surrounded by softness. The room is quiet. She has her stuffed animals, and feels warm. She also feels loved and her emotions are satisfied, so she's not looking to be comforted. Instead, she sleeps.

And you still don't know what she's thinking about or dreaming about! But you do know that you have a bond with her that is so strong it can't be broken by anything. She loves to feel "little", and craves your hands and your way of caring for her more than anything....possibly even more than chocolate.

She has a love for being a baby, for being placed in a diaper, and loved with all your heart, soul, mind, passion, and yes…you will eventually shed a tear or two.

The belief that we can't figure out girls only exists because we probably haven't taken the time to appeal to their emotions. Do I know what she's think? More often than not, Yes … I would. But I'd just be guessing some of the time, too. And that's okay because I'm still learning about her.

Reflections of the Root of the Bond

Friday evening. Work is done, and the car ride home produced a great feeling of long awaited freedom … the weekend at last. On my way home, I put in Tom Petty's Greatest Hits and mimicked Tom Cruise in "Jerry Maguire".

Pulling into the driveway, I was surprised to see her car was all ready there. She beat me home. A genuine smile of delight came across my face. We both were happy to get some free time. Above and beyond the work we had to do to make ends meet, we were two souls that always remembered what brought us together to begin with and what would keep us together for the rest of our lives … (but I'm getting ahead of myself a little.)

Now, where was I? …. Oh yes … The weekend, time to unwind. I walked into the house and saw a note sitting on the kitchen table with a bottle of wine and two glasses sitting next to it. Pinot Grigio: opened, poured and breathing. She was looking forward to tonight as much as I was. The note was very simple. "Wake me up … Daddy!" My face lit up with a smile again.

The hallway leading back to the bedroom was strewn with a pair of her nylons, her skirt, her blouse, her high heels, her bra, her underwear, a scarf, a bracelet, and a pair of earrings.

I walked back to the bedroom and slowly cracked the door open. There was warmth in the air that told me she was inside. She was the type of girl whose body temperature rose dramatically when she slept. (I don't know why it happened, but a warm girl on a cold night is truly precious.) The aroma of the room filled my senses. It's that sweet scent that follows a girl wherever she goes, and remains where she's been.

My eyes caught the site of a figure on the bed. Only her head was out of the blankets. She loved to sleep in the fetal position, and rarely shifted in her sleep at all. My heart began to beat at the pace of a racehorse. I was overcome with emotion. The girl I loved lay before me. It was the same emotion that overpowered me every time I saw her.

Her head faced away from me and all I saw was her beautiful long black hair. This morning she had straightened it, but often she would give herself curls. She liked the way her hair moved when it was curled, especially when I bounced her on my knee, or rocked her in my arms.

I knelt down beside the bed, and tenderly stroked the hair out of her face. She gently awoke, knowing I was coming for her. She stretched out of the fetal position. Turning her head towards me, our eyes met. I could feel my heart racing at full gallop again. She pulled her arms out from the covers. She had just applied red nail polish to her nails. Placing her hand over my heart, her face became flush with warmth and affection. My eyes redirected themselves to the pacifier in her lips. She winked at me.

I traced the outline of every feature of her face with my fingertips. She breathed softly behind her pacifier and closed her eyes. I delicately kissed her forehead. Her face lit up with a smile. She curled up her legs and began kicking in place as she giggled. It was her playful way of telling me she wanted to get up.

I heard a familiar noise under the covers. I peeled the covers off her. She was wearing one of my white button-down shirts, and a diaper which I knew she would be wearing. Placing a hand behind her head, I helped her sit up as I rose to my feet. She sat on her knees and threw her hands out and up, wanting to be lifted in my arms.

I had the pleasure of knowing her in two forms: "Big" and "Little". "Big" was the adult, the woman, the love and inspiration that I formed a union and life with. "Little" was the baby, the fun-loving side of her that needed to be nurtured and taken care of. When I first saw the pacifier in her lips, I knew instantly that she wanted to feel "little"…. at the moment, at least. But whether "big" or "little", she was who I cared about most.

I lifted her up into my arms. Her arms wrapped around my neck, her legs wrapped around my waist, we embraced and her body heat grew into me. I placed my hand on her diapered bottom for the sake of habit, but I all ready knew. (wink)

I carried her down the hallway, and into the living room. The last rays of sunlight were sneaking through the trees around the house and through the window. In an hour, it would be dark. I laid her on the couch, and tickled her ribs for a moment. She giggled again, then settled herself down and flat as I unfastened her diaper.

As I removed it and began to wipe her clean. She reached up and twisted my hair with her fingers. (It feels really good when she does that, I'll admit.) I lifted her bottom in the air and took a gentle stroke up each cheek with a wipe. I could tell her eyes were fixated on me.

I placed a new diaper beneath her and laid her bottom back down on it. The scent of powder permeated the air. As I drew the front of her diaper up and into place, she reached up to my face and began to touch it with her elegant fingertips. She was so gentle and caressing about. She would often stroke my face when I held her in my arms and fed her a bottle. My face fascinated her at those moments.

The button-down shirt came off, and a Yankees jersey went on her, Her choice, not mine.

Freshly cleaned and diapered, I lifted her up into my arms again. She rested her head on the side of my neck. She was feeling very "little" at this point. Getting her diaper changed often did that to her. We had found many different activities in a Daddy/BabyGirl relationship that would form a bond between us every time we did them. The diaper change was one of those bonding moments.

I held her in my arms for a moment rocking her back and forth. I all ready knew what she wanted next, but I wanted to take a moment to tell her how much she meant to me. “There’s never a moment that goes by without you in my thoughts, my senses, my soul and my heart,” I whispered in her ear.

I sat down on the couch and positioned her on my lap to rock her for a while. She lifted her head up, and allowed the pacifier to fall from her lips before turning my face towards her, closed her eyes, and kissed me softly. I put one arm around the back of her waist, and the other straight up her back while holding the back of her head in my hand.

We opened our eyes, and ended a sweet kiss. Tears had welled up in her eyes, and I was experiencing the same emotion. I rolled my fingers up and down her arms and legs. “Touch” was always a big thing with her. She loved the feeling of my hands on her skin. She devoted quite a bit of time (and lotion) to keeping her skin as soft and smooth as possible. When I touched her, I’m sure it felt very nice, but I think she also liked the fact that I noticed how soft her skin was.

In a sudden gesture of “little”, she crossed her eyes at me, and laughed. “You are the kindest guy I have ever known. You take care of me so tenderly. There’s nothing sweeter,” she said.

“Am I sweet like Pinot Grigio?” I asked, playfully.

She smiled, and stood up. “That’s not all,” she said while taking my hand and skipping like a little girl into the kitchen. She opened the oven and pulled out a delivery bag of some sort. I stood behind her, wrapped my arms around her waist, and rested my chin along the side of her neck.

She opened it and we looked in. “Thai food,” I said.

“Bring the wine and the glasses, Daddy, and follow me,” she said as she led me into the den. On the floor by the fireplace was a blanket with silverware, plates and candles. She had set up a blanket picnic….in our den. She lit the candles, opened the bag again and served it out. “So what is this we’re eating?” I asked.

She rattled it right off: “Curried vegetables and pork with rice noodles. It has bell peppers, asparagus, onions, sugar snap peas, fresh ginger … All kinds of healthy things.”

She lay on her tummy with her feet up in the air, and looked up at me. “Can I ask you a question, Daddy?”

“Absolutely.”

“When did you decide that you wanted me in your life?”

“When you go to bed thinking about someone and you wake up thinking about someone, and you think about her every moment in between, you realize that you've found someone that effects differently than anyone else. I never really had to decide. I all ready knew. What about you?"

While eating, she replied: "You make me feel good. Lots of people have made me feel pretty or sexy or happy, but when a girl finds a guy who makes her feel good all over, she's found a keeper…..and you let me be your BabyGirl. That's good, too."

She had cleared her plate except for the asparagus which she had pushed to the side. I set my plate down, and we both stared at each other. The flickering of the candles and the fireplace, providing the only light in the room, illuminated the face of this beautiful girl sitting in front of me… in a diaper and a Yankees jersey.

We said nothing, but we were still communicating with each other. The food we just ate, the wine we just drank, the fire-lit room we were in and the love we shared were putting the same want in our eyes.

"Come on. It's my turn to surprise you. We'll get the dishes later," I said as I leapt to my feet. She leaned over, blew the candles out, and hopped up. I took her by the hand, and began running to the back porch.

"I can't go outside in just my diaper!" she said with excitement. I grabbed a pair of sweat pants and her favorite pair of birken stocks. We got to the back porch. I sat on a chair, put her on my lap, the birken stocks on her feet, and the sweat pants on her legs.

Up we jumped, and off we went into the woods. She was trying to pull the sweat pants up the whole time we were running. Our foot race ended when we got to the tree line of the woods. Stopping to catch our breath, and to allow her time to pull the sweat pants up and tie them, I leaned up against a tree.

A little confused as to what was wrong, she kept trying to pull the sweat pants up, but had little success. Finally, she stopped trying and looked at me. "You grabbed a pair of your sweat pants, not mine," she said.

"Oh, sweetheart, I'm sorry. Should I go back and get another pair?" I asked.

"Naaaah!" she said playfully. "The only thing of mine that I need to be wearing is a diaper. I don't care what you dress me in. I'll love it all. So long as I'm with you."

Her speech was a little quick and slightly slurred. She wasn't able to drink much wine without it affecting her. Having caught her breath, I could see her mind was beginning to "wander" as to what we were going to do next. Her head lowered, and her eyes widened. She looked all around and then back to me with a grin. She didn't have to say it. I all ready knew.

"Hide and Go Seek?" I asked. She nodded as I gave her the pacifier and watched her run off to hide. She bounced as she ran, and her hair flopped around.

As a guy, the sight of a girl walking away from you or towards you is truly breath-taking. The way she carries herself, the way she moves - it's a very captivating moment to take in that vision of her, head-to-toe. It's another form of non-verbal communication. You can tell how she's feeling, perhaps even what's on her mind if you are passionate enough about her to get to know her that well.

I knew the odds of her hiding weren't going to be very good. Aside from dusk having set in, she had a gleaming white pacifier between her lips, and her diaper was not only visible because the sweat pants were too big for her waist, but it was also disposable (by her choice, but I whole-heartedly agreed) and it made that crinkling noise whenever she moved, crawled, walked, ran, jumped, anything.

I counted to ten, and then dashed into the trees. Shortly, I was no longer looking for her. I had found her. Now she was looking for me. This is what we did. She always wanted to be the one to hide, but after I counted and started looking for her, she wanted to try to find me. So I indulged her.

At first, she kept trying to look for me, but after a while she gave up. Because … she all ready knew she wasn't going to find me.

"Daddy?" she called out.

"Yes?" I replied from a distance.

"Are you about to sneak up on me?"

"Yes," I replied just a split second before I ran up behind her, grabbed her around the waist, lifted her in the air, and tickled her.

She howled with laughter. I set her down. She wrapped her arms around my body and laid her head on my chest. I returned the hug and kissed her on the forehead.

We had so many things in common which made bonding so easy for us. Even our heights were perfect for each other. I was 5' 11", and she was 5' 4". Which made the pheromones line up just right.

On the male body, pheromones are emitted all over from the skin. The highest concentrated area of pheromone emission on a guy is from his chest. The same is true of a female, but her highest pheromone emission zone is the top of her head. So, when we embraced, our noses lined up right with the other's "hot spot".

I reached down inside the sweat pants (which were barely hanging on to her waist) and put my hand on her diapered bottom. Patting her bottom was something that I liked to do anyway, but since she was in her "little" mode and wearing a diaper, it also served as a way to see if she needed her diaper changed. Because I all ready knew that she wouldn't tell me if she needed her diaper changed. Just so long as she could continue to wear it.

She folded her arms in front of her and curled up tightly in my chest. A diaper check served to make her feel really "little" at a moment's notice.

Just then, lightning illuminated the dark woods and thunder broke the sweet moment. Without any further warning, it began to pour rain. We dashed for the back porch, but she could only run so fast, and we were getting soaked. So I stopped in front of her, squatted slightly, and she jumped up on my back. Then we piggy-backed the yard. Getting under cover of the porch, we found relief in not having to dodge the raindrops anymore, but we were drenched just that quickly.

I looked at her and marveled over how, yet again, she was able to stop me dead in my tracks with the simplest thing. This time, it was her beautiful, long black hair that had become wet and was dripping. Knowing I was gazing at her, she shrunk her shoulders up and looked back up at me. The rain drops streaming down her face made her seem to glow.

And yet again, without saying a word the "eyes" returned from both of us. I reached out and pulled the waist string on the sweat pants. They fell off her and to the porch floor. She unbuttoned my shirt down to my chest, put her arms around me and gracefully drug her nails down my back. I lifted her up, walked into the house, and back to the bedroom. Piece-by-piece, we added another layer of clothing to the hallway rug. We got to the bedroom door. She reached out and opened it. I carried her in, turned out the light, and shut the door……………………

Sweet September (Part One)
The Morning

Sunday morning. Early September. I wake up without an alarm. This is a rarity because I am a heavy sleeper, and always need an alarm. But not on this day and the reason is clear. A smile comes across my face as I know what the day has in store. In the next room, there is a girl fast asleep who has stolen my heart and I absolutely love her for it. She and I have something in common that you don't always find easily.

Throwing the covers off my legs, I stood up. I'm not a morning person, but on this day I moved with purpose. I walked into the hallway and over to the next bedroom door. Placing my hand on the doorknob, I paused for a moment to recognize how lucky I was. In this room, there is a sleeping girl who shares a love for infantilism. For both of us, it's as pure and natural as it can be. It's role playing, but we never have to do much playing at all when it comes to us so effortlessly.

I turned the knob and slowly opened the door. The sunlight had made its way into the room and brought warmth with it. The scent in the air told me that there was a girl in the room. It's one of those little things that only a guy can truly appreciate. Whether it's a perfume, or a body lotion, or the scent of her hair, when you breathe it in, it brings every sense within you to life.

The room is set up exactly as she wants it. Pink everywhere. And the walls are covered with butterflies.

It's her dream nursery. From the closet in the corner filled with every bit of AB clothing you can imagine to the bookshelf, loaded with Dr. Seuss, Beatrix Potter, C.S. Lewis, Disney, you name it's there. The rocking chair sits next to the bookshelf, undisturbed and awaiting its next story time use. There is a net attached to the ceiling that covers one corner of the room. At this point, I would imagine there are probably over 100 stuffed animals in it, but I haven't counted recently.

Then there's the crib with the changing table next to it. From the doorway, I could see a mound of stuffed animals inside it. A soft white blanket lays heaped up in the middle, and beneath that blanket, she lies sleeping peacefully.

I walked up to the edge of the crib and looked down at her. Her eyes were so beautiful, and I couldn't wait to wake her up so she would open them and melt my heart. I reached up and turned off the nightlight above her crib. She was very frightened of the dark. I looked down at her again, and could feel my heart beating through my shirt. There she was. My AB Girl. The love of my life.

She always like to go to sleep while laying on her tummy, but somehow had wound up on her back. Her hair was beginning to fall out of its pigtails. It gave a slight look of bed head. I grinned as I gently lifted up her pink nightshirt. Hello Kitty, of course. I placed my hand on the front of her diaper. She had wet herself, but that was all.

I quietly lowered the side of the crib, and knelt down beside her. The sunlight streaming through into her crib touched golden beams on her face. She was so peacefully asleep, and I was in no hurry to wake her up, just yet. I could've knelt there and watched her dreaming face for hours. But she needed her diaper changed, and we had a busy day ahead of us.

This wasn't just any day. It was a very special day for her. From the moment I woke her up until the moment I put her to bed that night, this entire day she would spend as a baby, and every moment of this day I would be there to take care of her, to feed her, to bathe her, to hold her, to play with her, to love and to cherish everything about her and everything about her desire to be a baby.

This wasn't every day for us. We still had vanilla lives to lead outside of our ABDL ones. But today, she was going to be all baby, and I was going to make her happy.

I gently ran my fingers down the side of her face. She gently awoke and took in a deep breath before curling her arms up and stretching. She opened her eyes and looked up at the ceiling, then to either side of her on the crib mattress. She was looking for her pacifier, her cookie monster pacifier to be specific. She was never without it.

I parted her lips with that very pacifier. I had found it lying next to her, just moments before she rolled on top it. She looked over at me, and her beautiful brown eyes grew big and wide like she was about to burst with excitement.

When this girl smiled her entire face lit up, and behind a cookie monster pacifier, she was adorable.

She reached out to me with “Daddy, Pick Me Up!” I did just that, taking her up into my arms. She wrapped her arms around my neck and her legs around my waist, and I just stood there and we embraced for a few minutes. We needed to say good morning to each other and this is how we did it.

I kissed her softly on the forehead as she closed her eyes. “Good morning, Angel. Daddy loves you.” She touched my cheeks with both hands and then leaned back. I wrapped my arms around her legs, lightly patting her diapered bottom. She smiled brightly again behind her pacifier. And wrapped her arms around my neck again as I carried her over to the changing table.

I laid her down on the table, and she relaxed herself. The countless number of times she found herself there led me to put a whole bunch of neat stickers on the ceiling above for her to look at. They may have served as a pleasant distraction for her at one point, but now they just stood to playfully remind her that she was about to get her diaper changed.

I unfastened the tapes of her wet diaper, and folded the front down. In one quick motion, her legs and bottom went up into the air. Wiping her clean, and applying a little baby oil gel in the right places, she was lowered back down onto a new diaper that she didn’t even see me put underneath her. I had become somewhat of an engineer at doing this.

The feeling of a clean diaper was as much fun for her as the feeling of a wet diaper. She delighted that I took the time to make sure she was dry. If it was up to her, she probably wouldn't ever want her diaper changed. It took away from her time to be a busy babygirl, but she also delighted in me tending to her in this small but important way.

She and I had so much in common, and our love for the little details was a very big similarity. "All done!" I exclaimed.

She got up onto her knees on the table and stretched her arms out. Once again, I lifted her into my arms, this time patting her diapered bottom, a habit that I had. I carried her over to the crib so she could choose the stuffed animal she wanted to keep with her and her blanket, and out of the nursery we went, down the hallway into the kitchen. Along the way, we continued to say good morning to each other. (It was a lengthy process to say good morning, but one that we could never get enough of.) We touched noses "like de Eskimos do" she would always say. And then the blinking eyelash kisses "just like butterflies" she would always say. This girl loved butterflies.

I reached into the refrigerator and pulled out a small baby bottle of milk. I carried her into the living room, and sat on the sofa. I kept her on my lap, facing me. We looked at each other intently. (This was the laughing contest. We stared at each other and tried to get the other to laugh first.) I crossed my eyes for a second and she giggled. I took her blanket and covered and covered her head with it. She would take it off her head quickly, and then I would cover her with it again. This was our early morning version of peek-a-boo. We played it like this when we first woke up because neither of us were awake enough yet to play regular peek-a-boo.

I loved to catch her off guard with little tricks. I covered her head with the blanket, and as she pulled it off her head, I began bouncing my knees. Once again, it was the little things that brought a smile to her face and made her laugh. She did her best to hang on to my legs with her knees, but with a disposable diaper on and an inability to stop laughing, she never could hang on.

I scooped her up into my arms, sat back, laid her across my lap, and placed the baby bottle in her lips. She began to drink from it, and then reached up behind me to the back of the sofa. Suddenly, I felt her put my black Zorro hat on my head. I smiled at her and gave her a wink. She winked back and then nestled herself against my chest as she closed her eyes and drank from her bottle.

She stopped being silly for a while. When this happened, I knew that she wanted to feel “little”. So I gently rocked her back and forth and held her bottle to her mouth. Her left arm tightly hugged her teddy bear, and with her right hand she delicately ran her fingers up and down my arm. She was feeling very tiny and wanted to know where everything was around her. She didn't want anything to move. She didn't want anything to change. She wanted to feel safe and protected and cared for. It was what I always called her "little moments".

I stared down at her loving brown eyes. She looked back up at me, shyly, sweetly. And I said: "You are absolutely beautiful in every way. I love everything about you. How you crave the feeling of a soft blanket. The way you curl up in a ball when you watch cartoons. The fact that all the food on your plate has to be mixed together completely before you will eat it. The way a diaper makes you waddle when you try to walk. The wrinkling of your nose when you smell something that's bad. How you cock your head to the side when you make a decision. How ticklish your thighs are. How you respond to a gentle touch, soft words of kindness, and the chance to eat chocolate ice cream. And how your eyes tell me that this is exactly where you want to be."

I took the empty bottle from her lips. "And how your eyes tell me that you need to be burped in the worst kind of way," I said with a smile.

She puts her arms around me and I carried her into the kitchen. While making her breakfast, I gently bounced her up and down, and lightly patted her back. She rested her head on my chest, and sucked her thumb until…..

"BUURRPP!" She burped, and she burped loudly. She let out a sigh of relief, and smiled. "That felt really good!" she exclaimed.

“It sure sounded like it did,” I said while putting her breakfast in the microwave. “Sweetie, would you be a good girl and go pick out the bib you want to wear for breakfast?”

I set her down to her feet. Sheepishly, she scrunched up her shoulders and jumped up and down. “High chair?” she asked.

“Absolutely,” I answered as she hugged me. “Arms up.”

She raised her arms and I took her nightshirt off. “Go pick out your bib, sweetheart,” I said as I patted her on her diapered bottom.

She ran over to the drawer that had her bibs in it, and opened it. Almost like clockwork, she tilted her head to the side, trying to decide which one to wear. Finally, she picked up the yellow one with the big butterfly on it. She skipped back over, and handed it to me.

“What’s for breakfast?” she asked. I took her over to the microwave, and she looked through the glass to see what was inside. Her eyes lit up again as I put the bib around her neck, hoisted her in the air and carried her over to the high chair. She willingly climb into it, and I put the tray in place just as the microwave sounded it was done.

She looked down at the bib and lifted it up to look at the butterfly. She lowered her bib to see me putting a bowl of oatmeal on the tray in front of her. I pulled up a chair and sat next to her while swirling the oatmeal. She smiled and winked at me, knowing that I was going to spoon feed her. I winked back.

Scooping up the first spoonful, I asked: "Which will it be today, planes or trains?"

"You choose!" she said eagerly.

"Since you don't like to fly, we'll take a train instead." The first spoon began to chug-a-lug along through the air. She shyly scrunched up her shoulders and opened her mouth. She took the first spoonful in, and closed her lips around the spoon to get it all off. She smacked her lips, and awaited the next spoon. She ate that one the same way.

And through the feeding she began to get distracted from time to time. Her eyes would wander around the room, and she would occasionally bounce up and down in the high chair, but she was very much in a heavenly situation. And she was happy.

With oatmeal all over the face, she took in the last spoonful, and said: "All gone!" And as I took a wet washcloth to her face to clean her up, she crumpled up her nose. No baby likes to get her face wiped, of course. I took the bib off her neck, and unlocked the tray from the high chair. She put her arms up, waiting to be picked up. She knew what was coming next…one more bottle to wash breakfast down.

Up into my arms she went and she wrapped herself around me tightly while saying, “I love you, Daddy!” Tears welled up in my eyes, and I carried her into the living room again. I sat down and laid her across my lap. She took the next bottle into her mouth very eagerly.

And then she looked up at me with such a content look that all I could do was smile back at her. I couldn’t speak. Here was a girl who put all her trust in me to make her fantasy become the reality that it was. She opened her tender soul, hoping that I would take her most passionate secret and make her the happiest babygirl in the world. She was so sweet and so wonderful that I knew right then and there I would never again have to search for the things that my heart needed to survive.

She began to fall asleep again. She would fall asleep and wake up and continue to drink from her bottle. Then she would fall asleep again. And this continued until she fell asleep completely. I set the bottle aside and returned her pacifier to her lips. Her body relaxed into arms. Her cheeks began to release all stress, and I kissed her on the forehead while running my fingers along her eyebrows.

I held her in my arms like that for a while. Then she suddenly awoke, and sat straight up. She looked around for a moment and then down at her diaper. She looked at me sheepishly, and I winked at her playfully. “You ready for your bath time?” I asked.

She nodded excitedly. Up into my arms she went, one of her favorite places to be, and off we went to the bathroom. I sat on the toilet lid and put her on my knee. We both looked in the tub, and all of her bath toys were still in there from yesterday. (I spoiled this girl. I admit it.) No sooner had I plugged up the tub and turned the water on than she had all ready grabbed the bubble bath and poured a large amount into it.

The water level began to fill up. I took her pigtails out, letting her hair fall over her shoulders, and unfastened her wet diaper. She leaned over the edge of the tub, and began running her hands through the water, making the amount of bubbles grow.

I scooped her up in my arms, and began to lower her into the warm water. The moment I set her in the water completely, she began kicking her feet and splashing and went straight to her toys. I sat next to the tub for a little while and watched her enjoying her bubble castle.

Then she tired of playing and leaned back and closed her eyes. I picked up a wash cloth and bathed every inch of her body. Warm bath water and the touch of a soft cloth calmed her. She leaned her head back resting it on a towel I had placed in the edge. She took the pacifier out of her mouth, and said: “Don’t you ever wish I would take care of you?”

“You do take care of me,” I replied.

"How?" she asked while looking at me with a lively twinkle in her eyes.

"You are the sweetest girl in the world. You speak with love in your voice. You delight in the simplest things. Your fingertips feel like silk. Your eyes and your smile are so beautiful," I said as I lifted her out of the tub and into a towel on my lap. "And you want to be with me."

She smiled at me warmly and lovingly, and put the pacifier back into mouth as I carried her into nursery. I put her down on her feet and began to dry her off with the towel, saving her hair for last. "What color of t-shirt do you want to wear?" I asked as I laid her down on the carpet.

She laid her head on the carpet and pointed to the closet. I walked over and opened it up. "A pink one!" she exclaimed.

I grinned; knowing that pink was always her choice. So I grabbed a pink t-shirt off the shelf closet, and said, "Arms Up."

She sat up and raised her arms to the sky. I brought it down over her head and hands and over her body. I pulled her out of her shirt and let it lay on her shoulders to dry. She crawled over to her doll house, and I followed after her, picking her up and carrying her over to the changing table.

“Not yet, Princess,” I said as I laid her on her back and put her in a diaper. “I have a question for you.”

She looked up at me with wonder. I opened up the book I had hiding behind my back and read from it. “Do you like green eggs and ham?”

Her face lit up like a Christmas tree. She sat up and jumped off the table, grabbing me by the hand and taking me over to the rocking chair, which she called the read’n chair. I took a seat and she sat on my lap, resting her head on my chest as I read Green Eggs and Ham. As I read it, she recited the words with me. I finished the whole book and she made me read it again. I offered to read it backwards, but she shook her head no and called me silly.

I kept her on my lap and took a brush to her hair, returning the pigtails that she so dearly loved. And as I was doing this, I realized that the little things that she delighted in so very much, I was beginning to delight in as well, just in a different way. I loved her like no other, and it filled me with such a warm feeling to make her laugh and to put that magnificent, adoring smile on her face. Pigtails did that very thing to her. Maybe it was because she liked them, or maybe it was because I was the one who put her hair up like that. Either way, she was happy.

“You wanna watch some cartoons?” I asked.

“Yep!” she said enthusiastically as she leaped off my lap and ran out of the nursery towards the living room. I sat there for a moment and smiled at watching her trying to waddle/run in her diaper. It was an endearing and sugary sweet site to behold. I leaned forward to stand up when I heard her running back down the hallway towards me in the nursery. She ran back in, grabbed me by the hand, yanked me up out of the chair, and pulled me in the hallway, at which point she let go of my hand, went sprinting down the hallway towards the TV room and leapt into the air, landing on the couch.

The TV was on and she was all ready into an episode of Mickey's Playhouse. I walked into the kitchen, and began cleaning up the high chair and kitchen floor. Every few minutes I would glance back in the living room to see if she was okay. And she was mesmerized by the TV. Mickey Mouse has that power.

"You want Macaroni for lunch, sweetheart?" I asked from the kitchen.

"Yes! But de yellow ones, not de orange," she replied.

"Okay. Velveeta then, Not Kraft," I said with a smile. I began to prepare it, still smiling about how particular she was. She would only eat certain things. Period. That's it. Some things I had to give in on. Honestly, I didn't mind. For as much as I took care of her, she had me wrapped around her finger. She knew how to get what she wanted when she wanted it. And I didn't mind that either. I would have it no other way.

Loading up a bowl with macaroni and cheese (the yellow, not the orange!) and placing it in the freezer for a moment to cool down, I called out to her. “Lunch is ready! Is there any BabyGirl nearby who might want some yellow macaroni and cheese?”

I heard her hop up to her feet and run into the kitchen like an excited two year old. She crashed into me, hugging me, and exclaiming, “Me!”

I pretended I see her, and kept looking into the living room. “Anyone? Anyone at all?” I said.

She started jumping up and down in front of me. “Me, Daddy! Me! Me! Me!” she said.

I looked down at her with surprise. “Well when did you come in here?”

“I came in when you called,” she said while lifting her arms up.

I took her t-shirt off, and attached a bib. (Hey, I’ve learned.) Up into my arms she went and she dropped her pacifier in my shirt pocket for safe keeping. I carried her over to the high chair, and she sat in it very politely and waited for the tray to be put in front of her before she started bouncing up and down. I went over to the fridge and took the bowl out of the freezer. It had cooled down enough for her now. She liked to eat macaroni with her fingers. It was another one of many thousands of adorable things that she liked to do.

I set it the bowl down on the tray in front of her, and watched her fold her hands and bow her head. She always said a silent prayer. Except in the mornings. Sometimes she would honestly forget or she wouldn't be awake enough. But it was very much important to her. I was glad she and I shared that conviction as well.

She leaned over the bowl and started taking handfuls of it and devouring it. This was one of her favorite meals. And with each handful of it, her face became more and more covered with cheese. She had cheese on her hands and part way up her arms by the time she finished and leaned back to burp. And her burps were adorable, too. She tried to belch loudly, but just didn't have it her. She was a girl and even when she tried to be ungirly about things, she was still a girl.

I put the bowl in the sink, and took a washcloth to her arms and face, and just like at breakfast, she hated it, but it had to be done. Besides, Daddy wasn't going to let her out of that high chair until she was cleaned up. She eventually gave in and let me clean her face. I took the tray off and then her bib from her neck. As if we had down this many times before (because we had), she instinctively put her arms up for her t-shirt to go back on.

I picked her up and carried her into the living room. She reached into my shirt pocket and found her pacifier. I lifted her up, and asked: "Play Dough or Coloring?"

She cocked her head to the side, trying to decide. "Coloring!" she finally shouted out.

I set her down on the living room rug and she crawled over to the basket alongside the couch. She pulled out 12 coloring books, and an enormous handful of crayons, throwing it all over the rug and getting right to it. I sat down on the couch and turned the TV on.

"Wuh yachin', Daddy?" she asked not looking up from her coloring.

"The Chiefs," I answered.

"Fooooooo Ball," she said.

This was opening Sunday for the NFL, that horrid wait since the Superbowl in January was over, and I was eternally grateful that she didn't fuss when I watched football. It was something that I really wanted to do, much like her desire to be a babygirl. And I had learned to not get so shoutingly excited during the football games. I call it a necessary agreement.

She entertained herself with her coloring books, and I would occasionally hear her talking to herself. From the floor, I would hear, "Wu Not eat it wit a fox. Wu not eat it in u box." She eventually began to tucker out a little, crawled over to the couch and up on my lap. She curled up in the fetal position and began to fall asleep. It was soon time for her nap, so this wasn't a little cat nap. It would soon be crib time.

I held her for a while until she was fast asleep. Checking her diaper once more before taking her back to the nursery, I slowly stood up, and carried her back the hallway. She was out like a light on my shoulder. I turned the lights off in the nursery, and closed the curtains with one hand, being careful not to wake her. I walked carried her over to her crib, lower the side of the crib, turned her nightlight on, and very delicately laid her down in the crib on her tummy.

As I stood up, she awoke and began to cry lightly. "Hey, I'm right here," I whispered to her softly.

"I don't wanna go to bed," she fussed as I pulled the blanket over her body. "I don't wanna go to bed."

I leaned in towards her face, put her pacifier in her mouth, and kissed her on the forehead. "Shh-shh-shh," I whispered. "You've got a busy day ahead of you and it's only just begun. It's time to rest."

In a matter of seconds, she was asleep. I raised the side of her crib, and quietly walked over to the door. I glanced back at her sleeping, and then shut the door.

Sweet September (Part Two)
The Afternoon

I walked back to the laundry room, and …. (yes, I do laundry!), and picked up her diaper bag and a set of clothing. She and I were going to go on a trip that afternoon. She knew nothing about it. Her nap times were the perfect opportunities to prepare a surprise. I knew when I woke her up and told her we were going on a trip, she would become so excited that I would have to calm her down, and there would be no time to pack a bag.

Every trip we took, even just a small one, out and about, she would find some way to make her clothes dirty. Sometimes I believed she did this purposefully just so I would change her clothes. So I learned that I always needed a second outfit on hand. In the laundry room there was a bib overall shorts outfit that I washed a few days ago. It would do the job, and she would be very happy to wear it. I was able to fit it into the diaper bag with a little room left over. So I prepped a few snacks and drinks to take and left them in the fridge until we were closer to leaving.

Ah yes. A little time for Daddy, and what did I do? I sat down on the couch, put my Zorro hat on, and watched "The Mask of Zorro" because….that's what I do. I certainly wasn't going to watch the sequel to it. Everything that Steven Spielberg did to make "The Mask of Zorro" such a success was tarnished by the movie's follow up.

But I never really had time where I relaxed completely. And honestly, I don't think I wanted to be that relaxed. So…five minutes into the movie, I paused it so I could check on her in the nursery, and wash some dishes. I was very happy to give up my freedom to do this. And she stayed on my mind. Soon I would wake her up, and I knew what she would want to eat…..grapes. She loved grapes. Frozen grapes were a real treat. So I got some frozen grapes from the freezer and put them in a bowl, setting it on the couch in the living room. Next to it, I set a hair brush. She loved to have her hair brushed out. When I did this, I looked over at one of her stuffed animals on the couch. I smiled for a moment, and thought about how much she meant to me.

The loved I felt for her was unlike anything else I had ever felt. It was a combination of paternal pride and paternal love added into a genuine guy's affection for a girl that never leaves his thoughts. I could "check" on her in her crib, or I could just crack the nursery door open and watches her sleeping. Her body lays flat to the mattress. She's just a little bump under the covers. Her body rises and lowers ever-so-slightly with each breath, and when she resituates in her sleep, she lets out a tiny little sigh as she relaxes into a new position. The noise her disposable diaper makes when she shifts her hips seems to echo in my ears like the sweet sound of rainfall. She can never escape the beauty she possesses, even in her slumber.

An hour came and went and this girl who didn't want to sleep was still resting calmly like a baby. I quietly walked over to the crib, lowered the side, knelt down beside her just as when I woke her up that morning. I peeled the cover off of her body, and made a discovery. She would need a diaper change, very soon. The scent in the air told me she had pooped. And past experience had taught me to handle this situation delicately, but also quickly.

I grabbed a diaper and some wipes from the changing table, and began to unfasten her diaper in the crib. She was laying on her tummy. I tried to peel back the tapes on her diaper quietly. If she were to have awoke with a load in her diaper, she would have squirmed as well as been upset. Every tape sounded like a buffalo stampede of noise running through the room. I was sure she would wake up. And of course, the diaper I put on her was the kind with 3 tapes per side, so this was taking forever.

After what seemed like ten minutes of unfastening, I lowered the back of her diaper down very carefully. Luckily she was asleep on her tummy and her legs were bent and parted a little. So I had at least some room to work with here. I took the wipe to her tush. Thinking she would wake up as I did this, I prepared to stop her from startling into movement. That might have created a mess in the crib. But she didn't wake up, and was now clean.

Proudly I stood up, and took a moment to simply be proud that I was able to unfasten her poopy diaper and wipe her clean without stirring her. As I stood there, being proud……she shifted her legs. A look of silent panic came over my face as she rolled on her side. Then, at that moment, I knew there were greater forces than I out there, who were trying to help me. She rolled on her side and off her diaper completely, which made it easy to roll it up and get it out of the crib.

It was at this moment, when the "coast was clear" that she woke up, very calmly. She looked up at me and smiled, reaching out for me to pick her up. It was at the moment I picked her up that she realized she wasn't wearing a diaper. In my arms, she looked at me confused, then down at her bare bottom, then down at the rug of the nursery, then back to me. I could tell she was really trying to figure out what happened to her diaper. She was wearing it when she went to sleep. It stood to reason that she would be wearing it when she woke up. She looked inside my shirt pocket, and I started to laugh. This was hysterical to see her trying to wake up and trying to figure out this mystery.

She shrugged her shoulders and laid down on my chest. She put her head on my shoulder and felt the material of my shirt with her fingers. I walked over to the changing table, laid her down, and put her in a diaper. I picked her up, carried her out of the nursery, and down the hall to the living room. All along the way, she would look down at her diaper. Then she would look away. Then she'd look down at her diaper, wondering if this one was going to magically disappear, too.

When we got into the living room, she saw the bowl of grapes. I sat down on the couch and put her on my knees, facing her towards me. She grabbed the bowl and began eating the grapes, stuffing six of them in her mouth at once. Her cheeks puffed out from the grapes, and she tried to smile, but obviously couldn't. Instead, she laughed. I sat there with a grin on my face.

"I have a surprise for you," I said as I took the hair ties out of her hair, letting her pigtails down.

"Mur Graps?" she mumbled with a full mouth, followed by more laughter and a snort which only made her laugh more.

"Chew, BabyGirl," I jokingly instructed as I picked up the hair brush and began the feather her hair down over her shoulders. She began to chew the grapes, and closed her eyes, anticipating how good it was going to feel to have her hair brushed.

I began to slowly brush out every lock of her beautiful hair. She gracefully reached up to touch my face with her fingertips. She opened her eyes and looked at me. "Thank you for being so sweet to me," she said while lightly biting her lower lip.

"Thank you for owning my heart and never leaving my soul," I said as I put the brush down and kissed her forehead. As I did this, she touched my cheeks with her fingertips again. She collapsed into my chest and hugged me. I wrapped my arms around her and gave her the diapered bottom pat. She smiled sweetly.

“Thank you for that, too,” she said softly. Then suddenly, she sat up. “What’s the surprise?”

“A trip,” I said.

“Where we goin’, Daddy?” she asked with a bounce of excitement.

“It wouldn’t be a surprise if I told you,” I said in a sly manner. “But,” I began while pointing to the clothing I had on the other end of the couch. “We need to get you dressed, don’t we?”

She crawled over to the clothes, took her t shirt off in a flash, got into the yellow summer dress, slip the sandals on her feet, crawled back over to me and plopped back down on my lap.

“Ready to go, Daddy!” she exclaimed as she stood up and grabbed my hand lifting me to my feet as well.

“Where’s my diaper bag?” she said as she headed for the door. I picked up the bag, and she practically ran us to the door. Then she stopped, and began to buckle at the knees. I grabbed her before she fell.

“What’s wrong?” I said dropping the bag and holding her to my chest.

“Nothing. It’s the first time I walked today,” she said. “I bet there’s a bag of drinks and treats you almost forgot in the fridge.”

"The drinks and treats can wait. Are you all right?" I said getting ready to abandon this trip.

"I'm fine!" she said. "I got light-headed. I've been crawling around all day."

She ran over to the fridge, got the bag of treats and snacks, ran back to me, picked up the diaper bag I dropped, put everything in my hands and went to the door.

"I know you're not going to tell me where we're going, but I want clues, she said opening the door.

"Okay, I'll give you clues on the way there," I said following her out and heading to the car.

Sweet September (Part Three)
The Trip

We got in the car, and I drove down the road with a big grin on my face. I didn't say anything. She sat there patiently, until finally she blurted out: "Clues! Clues! Clues!"

"All right, all right," I started. "Where we are going, the sky's the limit."

"Outer space!" she guessed lightheartedly.

"No. That would be a little beyond the limit," I responded.

"Are there animals there?" she inquired.

"Yes, but it's not a zoo. I would not go there in a shoe. I would not go there in a box. I would not go there with a fox….."

"More Clues. Less Seuss, Daddy."

"You can almost touch the clouds, and there are trees for miles."

"Is it a park?"

“Yes. See, you didn’t need the clues. It was a matter of time before you figured it out. Yes, Nittany Park. Mount Nittany, actually. ”

“What does Nittany mean?”

“It’s a type of lion that used to live here. It’s also a Native American word. ”

“What does it mean in Niv American?” she began to say in a very child-like manner.

Realizing she wanted to feel little, I obliged. “I don’t know. I guess we’ll find out when we get there. I also hear there’s a legend of Mount Nittany,” I said.

“”Really?”

“And we’ll find that out, too, when we get there,” I said as I began to lay it on thick. “I also hear there is a legend of Mount Nittany.”

“A scary legend?”

“No. The legend of how Mount Nittany was formed,” I said as we pulled into the park.

We pulled into a parking space, and directly in front of us was a bronze statue of a lion. It wasn’t as big as the one on Penn State Main Campus, but her eyes became glued to it. She got out of the car, and ran up to it. I got out of the car, grabbing the diaper bag, and following after her.

She walked all around the statue with eyes as big as could be. “And dats a ninny lion?” she asked.

“Yes, sweetheart. There used to be lions just like that one all over this mountain range at one point,” I answered, taking her hand and leading her down the trail.

“Where’d they all go?” she asked innocently.

“Probably away from us, as fast as they could,” I answered.

At the base of the trail was a plaque. We walked up to it, and I said, “And here it is. The Legend of Mount Nittany.”

“Read it to me, Daddy,” she asked sweetly as she brought my arms over her shoulders. And pressed herself against my body.
“Please?”

“Certainly, Sweetheart,” I replied as I read the word on the plaque:

“The Legend of Mount Nittany: Nit-A-Nee, which means ‘single mountain,’ was an Indian maiden whose lover, Lion's Paw, was killed...

Nit-A-Nee enfolded him into her arms and carried his still erect body back to a place in the center of the Valley where she laid the strong Brave in his grave and built a mound of honor over his strength.

On the last night of the full moon, after she had finally raised the last of the soil and stone over his high mound, a terrible storm came up unleashing itself with thunder and lightning and the wailing of a horrendous wind from the depths of the earth. Every Indian in the Valley shuddered and all eyes were directed to the Indian Brave's high mound upon which the strong maiden Princess Nit-A-Nee was mounted with arms outstretched to touch the sources of the lightning bolts in the sky.

Through the night they watched with awe as the Indian Brave's burial mound grew and rose into a Mountain penetrating the center of the big valley between the two legs of the Tussey and Bald Eagle Ridges. When the dawn finally came, a huge Mountain was found standing erect in the center of the Valley.

And that's all it says. Let's see where the trail takes us."

So we started walking up the trail. I put my hand behind her back, and we skipped a few steps, but I could see she was bored by it. So I placed my hand on her diapered bottom to "check". She looked up at me and a big grin came across her face. She smashed herself into the side of my body like a shy four-year-old.

"You have no idea what's ahead of us, do you?" I asked.

She looked ahead, and said: "Trees."

I let out a laugh at her quick, yet honest answer. "Yes. There are a lot of trees," I stated while still laughing, "but looked!"

I stopped and pointed off to the left. "What's under those trees?"

Her eyes grew great big and wide once again. She leapt into my arms, and hugged my neck while exclaiming: "Swings! Will you push me in one of them?"

"Will you be good girl and hold on tightly to the swing if I do?" I playfully asked while carrying her over to the swing set.

"Yep!" she cried out while leaping out of my arms and running over to the swing.

I stopped dead in my tracks and put a fat-lipped, sad face on. She looked back at me, rolled her eyes up in her head, ran back to me, grabbed me by the hand, and ran us back to the swing. "Come on, Daddy!" she said while laughing.

She jumped into the swing without a moment to lose. "High. I wanna go really, really, really, really, really high," she said with excitement.

"How many reallys was that?" I asked.

She counted out the number on her fingers, then showed me her hand. "Five," she answered.

"I don't know," I said.

"Why? What's wrong?"

"BabyGirls should never go higher than four reallys. This many," I said while showing her four fingers.

She touched her left pointer finger to her lip, and went deep into thought. Then, she thought of a comeback line. She snapped her fingers and said, "But good BabyGirls are allowed to do five reallys high. And I said I would be good. So five it is," she answered with sincerity.

"That's true. I can't argue with that," I said admitting defeat. (-wink-)

Content that she had won, she sat straight up in the swing, grabbed the chains on each side, and readied herself to be pushed. I grabbed the swing on either side, pulled her way back up high (five reallys high, mind you, not four!), and I let her go. She swung through the air like a bird. And with each pass, I heard her laughter increasing.

Her hair fluttered in the wind, and the sun shined through the trees and down over her dress with golden beams. She was an angel that seemed to have wings all of the sudden. Her smile, which always lit up her entire face and the room she was in, was now lighting up everything around us. Her laughter echoed up and down the mountainside.

When I slowed her up, and stopped the swing, I could tell she loved it. She got off the swing and embraced me. “I love you

Daddy. I love you so much,” she said. “Can I have a Coke?”

“You certainly may,” I said while opening the diaper bag.

She reached in, grabbed a Coke, and handed it to me with the most precious ‘Please!’ face in the world. I smiled, and opened the Coke. She grabbed it, chugged the thing right down, and then let out a burp.

“Do you feel better?” I asked as I took the empty can and put it back in the bag.

“Uh-huh,” she responded as we started up the trail.

“You know what’s so wonderful about BabyGirls?” I asked.

She smiled. “Tell me,” she said.

"They're emotional. They just want to be loved. They want to feel loved and they want to know that they will always be loved.

They want to be taken care of and they never want to feel like they are a burden. They never are a burden, but they never let a moment go by where they don't cherish how someone makes them feel."

She smiled sweetly.

I continued on. "Her smile makes her beautiful. Her dimples and tiny nose make her adorable. Her pigtails make her happy. Her pacifier makes her comfortable. Her clothing makes her feel little. Her bib tells her it's okay to be messy. Her crib tells her it's time to settle down. Her diaper makes her feel like a baby. Her stuffed animals surround her and she hugs them all. And her Daddy makes her the happiest BabyGirl in the world."

She smiled a lot wider and added, "and her Daddy knows best. She wants to make him happy, too."

"She does. Every morning she wakes up, and opens her beautiful eyes and looks at me with a burning love I can't describe. She may be a little baby, but her effect is really huge."

"I don't ever want to know anything other than the way you make me feel, Daddy."

"My promise, BabyGirl: You never will."

We walked up to another plaque alongside the trail. "Your turn to read," I said as I walked up behind her, wrapped my hands around her, and put my chin on the top of her head.

She put her hands on my arms and leaned her head back on my chest. "Too many words," she said.

"As you wish, my dear," I said as I began to read the plaque:

"Kalmia latifolia, commonly called Mountain-laurel or Spoonwood, is a flowering plant in the family Ericaceae, native to the eastern United States, from southern Maine south to northern Florida, and west to Indiana and Louisiana.

It is an evergreen shrub growing to 3-9 m tall. The leaves are 3-12 cm long and 1-4 cm wide. Its flowers are star-shaped, ranging from red to pink to white, and occurring in clusters. It blooms between May and June. All parts of the plant are poisonous. Roots are fibrous, matted.

The plant is naturally found on rocky slopes and mountainous forest areas. The plant often grows in large thickets, covering large areas of forest floor. In North America it becomes a tree on the mountains of the Carolinas but is a shrub further north."

"Mow-In Florah," she gibbered out.

I looked around. Nobody was anywhere to be seen. So I decided to get silly. “Hey, do you wanna see what this park looks like at a really fast speed?” I asked.

“Huh?” she asked, quite bewildered.

I tickled her sides and she howled with laughter until she broke free and began running away from me through the forest. I stood there for a moment, giving her a head start, and then bolted after her. I chased her for a while, waiting until we ran through an area without tree cover.

When we found a clearing, and caught up to her, grabbed her lifted her in the air, and placed her on her back on the ground. While she tried hard to fight me off with her hands, she couldn’t stop laughing long enough to stop me from flipping her dress up and blowing raspberries on her tummies. She kicked her legs up and down, and I eventually let her flip me over on my back.

While sitting on me, she finally had a moment to catch her breath and try to recover from laughing. “That wasn’t fair,” she laughingly stated in a breathless tone. “”I’m shorter than you and I have sandals on, and I’m wearing a diaper and I’m a babygirl…”

I sat up, holding her to me, and kissed her very softly and quickly on the lips. “And I love you for being all of that and so much more.”

We sat there for a moment gazing into each other's eyes. "Do you remember the first time we met?" she asked.

"As if it were yesterday, Princess," I fondly recalled. "We met at that little coffee shop you loved just on the edge of your hometown. You were so nervous to meet me, but you were beautiful in that dress, and your face was even more beautiful than the pictures you sent me. You were a little late, and you ran in with serious concern that I had left. I would have stayed there all night waiting for you. But then we saw each other, and didn't it feel like the world stopped moving for a second?"

"Yes," she responded in a tiny voice as she stared deep into my eyes.

"We didn't say anything at first, did we. No. There weren't any words that the moment needed or required. I don't think I could have spoken at that moment. We knew so much about each other that the next step was to meet each other."

"I remember running into your arms, and how warm your body felt. How good it felt to be in a Daddy's arms. I wasn't nervous after that. I had to meet you to know if I would feel the same as when we spoke, and I did."

I kissed her on the forehead again, and she got off my chest and laid next to me. We looked up at the evening sky. There was plenty of sunlight left to the day, and the clouds were still bright white.

"What do you see in those clouds?" she asked.

"More clouds," I replied. "How about you? When a girl, with all the love in the world for little things in her heart, looks at those clouds, what does she see?"

I looked over at her. She looked at every cloud in the sky, then spoke: "I see rivers and streams. Lakes and Seas. Oceans and Waterfalls."

"And rainbows?" I asked softly, knowing why she was saying those things.

She looked back at me with tears in her eyes. "Yes," she said very quietly.

"Shh," I said very softly as I wipe a tear off her cheek. "It's okay. I am always going to take care of you."

I reached my hand underneath her, and found that her dress was soaked. I stood up, unbuttoned my shirt, lifted her to her feet, wrapped the shirt around her waist and we began walking back down the trail.

"Why were you crying?" I asked.

"You're so kind to me," she said. "Sometimes it makes me cry."

She paused for a moment and then continued, "Do you know what's so wonderful about Daddies?"

"Tell me," I said.

"They care for you in a way that you never get cared for again for the rest of your life. Their voices are soft, and their hands are strong, yet gentle. You can collapse in their arms, and they will be there to catch you. You can fall to pieces and they will glue you back together, stronger than before. They make everything that seems like such a big problem seem like a little one and then they fix it so you can forget about it. If you feel grumpy they will make you happy."

She paused for a moment to clear the lump in her throat before continuing: "And if you wet yourself and if by chance you soak your dress in the process, a Daddy will give you the shirt off his back to make you feel better."

She pressed herself up against my side and put her head on my shoulder as we walked the rest of the way to the car. We were the only ones left in the park as dusk approached. I unlocked the car and opened the back door on the driver's side. She took a seat and lifted the dress off her body. In a flash, I pulled the extra set of clothes out of her diaper bag, and had the baby-t over her head and on her body.

She layed flat on the back seat. I sat alongside her on the edge, handed her favorite teddy bear to her, put her pacifier in her mouth, and began to unfasten her diaper. In one quick motion, her legs and bottom went up in the air, I wipe her clean and positioned the new diaper under her.

Lowering her back down onto the diaper, I could see from the look on her face that she was feeling very small and little now. I obliged what her heart was longing for at that moment.

"You've been a very good girl on this trip," I said as I fastened her new diaper into place.

She looked at me with wonderment of what I was planning next. I took the sandals off her feet, and placed them on the floor of the car with her diaper bag. It was time for a heart-pounder of a moment for both of us. For as much as it got our hearts pounding, what I did next was a rush and a thrill and a craving as well.

I picked her up in my arms, lifted her out of the car, and carried her over to throw away her wet diaper in the trash can about 30 feet away. Being carried like a baby, wearing a baby-t, a disposable diaper, with bare feet, and with a pacifier in her mouth, she felt like a baby from the tip of her head to the tip of her toes.

At first, she sat up looking around to figure out where I was carrying her. Then she became overwhelmed with that baby feeling and she rested her head on my shoulder. She clutched her teddy bear in one arm and reached up with her other hand to cling to the collar of my t-shirt.

As I walked us back to the car, I spoke softly into her ear. “You’ve been a very good baby girl today, too.”

A grin came over her face as I patted her diapered bottom. This sent shivers up her spine and she began to giggle as I kept trying to touch the tip of her nose with my pointer finger. I opened the driver’s door, got in the car and laid her down on the front seat with her head in my lap. Before we pulled away, I covered her body with her blanket.

As we drove off. She shifted and laid on her back so she could look straight up at me as I drove. I looked down at her, and asked:

“Are you tired?”

She shook her head no.

“How do you feel about one more trip? We’ll have to put some pants on you first.”

She sat up, put her legs in an Indian style, and waited.

“Oh! You’re waiting for a clue?” I asked as she nodded. “Let’s see. Where we are going next, there will be lots of people, and lots of fun things to do, but no pacifiers allowed.”

She smiled, and removed her pacifier from her mouth. “What about sweet little baby girls and their daddies?”

"That will be fine. Come here. I'll whisper in your ear where we're going and you tell me if you want to go." I said.

She crawled over to me and leaned her ear in to listen. I whispered it to her, and her eyes lit up.

"I'll take that as a yes," I said. "Now buckle yourself up, Sweetheart. We'll be there soon."

Sweet September (Part Four) The Conclusion

"What kind of rides do they have there?" she asked.

"I guess the usual kind of carnival rides, but this is one of those traveling deals. I'm sure it won't be massive roller coasters and waterslides, but they'll have a lot of other things to do," I replied. "Listen, before you get buckled up, reach in the backseat and grab the diaper bag. I have another set of clothes in there for you."

She leaned over the front seat and reached down to the back floor trying to pick up the bag, but she could quite reach it. So she stood up on the front seat and leaned the top half of her body over it to finally get the bag. As she was doing this, I glanced over at her, and what I saw was a pair of bare feet standing on tip toes, and a pair of naked legs stretching up to a diapered bottom.

She was really having trouble getting at the diaper bag. It was too precious and perfect of a moment for me to let it get away.

I reached over with my right hand and grabbed her one leg at the back of the thigh, and I began to tickle her. Her legs, especially her inner thighs were extremely sensitive and ticklish. She broke out into laughter, and tried to kick her legs to free herself from my grasp, but she couldn't. Finally, she pulled herself back up with the diaper bag in hand and sat back down, red-faced from laughing and of course from being upside down.

"Did you find the diaper bag?" I asked with a grin.

"Yes," she said amusingly. "And somebody was tickling me and making me laugh."

"Really? I didn't see anyone doing that."

"He's right there," she said while pointing to the rear view mirror.

"He's not a bad looking guy," I said admiring myself in the mirror.

"No, he's not bad looking at all," she said while leaning in and kissing my cheek. "And he's a fun Daddy, too."

She set the diaper bag on the passenger side floor in the front, and opened it. She pulled out the yellow overall shorts I packed for her, and smiled.

"How did you know?" she asked.

"How did I know what?" I replied.

"How did you know that this is exactly what I wanted to wear right now?"

"I have my sources, but I'll never tell."

At the first stop light, she put her legs up in the air and slid the overalls over them. When she got them up her legs, she wiggled to get them up the rest of her body, and then connected the bib top at the shoulders. She sat back up and took a moment to relax after having had to squirm so much. She noticed me watching and looked over at me with a smile.

"That was mighty impressive," I said with a smile.

She continued on, bending her knees and putting her feet on the seat to get her socks and shoes on. And as she slid her second shoe on, she looked out the front window and there in front of us, filling the night time sky, was a festival with rides and food and everything you would want to see.

I pulled into the grass area designated for parking, and her eyes were glued to the ferris wheel. She pointed to it, and said: "Can we go on dat, Daddy?"

She looked at me for my response. I smiled with every bit of love for her simple, honest question. I had the hesitation to say yes for only a moment, because she was extremely afraid of heights. But I looked in her eyes and I all ready knew that the answer had to be yes.

Her eagerness to jump up and down was evident, but she patiently sat there on her knees, waiting for my answer. I touched her cheek with my hand, and stroked it. "Yes, Sweetheart. If you really want to, and I will go on it with you."

She wrapped her arms around my neck, and said, "Thank you, Daddy. Thank you so much."

Those words brought tears to my eyes. I opened the car door and got out of the car. She got out right behind me holding my hand. I leaned back into the car, reached across the front seat to get the diaper bag when she pulled me back out.

"I promise I won't need my diaper changed while we're here," she said with certainty in her voice.

I smiled playfully. "And when you do need it changed, we'll simply come back out to the car and change you. Deal?" I said.

"Deal," she repeated.

"Okay. No diaper bag then," I said, while picking her up and sitting her on the hood of the car so I could tie her shoelaces.

We walked to the entrance, and her eyes went back to the ferris wheel. In particular, she looked at the top of the wheel. "It's so high!" she said with nervous excitement. "How high is it?"

"Let's go find out," I said as I paid for our entrance, and led her to the ferris wheel.

Her steps were reluctant. They were …….baby steps, if you will. This was a challenge that excited her, but still scared her a little.

As we got closer to it, she began to squeeze my hand tighter and tighter. Our time standing in line for it wasn't all that long, thankfully. A long wait may have given her time to back out. She had the courage to face her fear of heights but it was still a fear that controlled her.

Our turn arrived. The wheel stopped spinning, and the attendant opened the carriage for us. Her steps were so gentle and careful. It was almost as if she was just learning to walk. She stepped inside and sat next to me, smashing her body up against me. The attendant closed the door, stepped back, and up and away we went.

As we rose higher, she would bury her face in my chest. As we descended she would look back out again. With each revolution of the wheel, her grip of my arm and body became a little less tight. I began to feel the blood flowing back into my arm. Then, the wheel stopped with us at the very top. Anyone who has ever been stopped at the top of a ferris wheel knows what happens. We stopped with a quick motion, and the carriage swung back and forth a little. She tightened her grip of my arm back up, buried her whole face in my chest, and held her breath.

"BabyGirl, we're at the top!" I said, encouraging her to look out. "You did it. You made it to the top…….It's an incredible view. Take a look, Sweetheart. You're going to love it."

She looked up at me, and then ever-so-slowly turned her head out. We could see for miles up there. Every little light in every window in houses, every street lamp, people walking around, cars driving by. Then I looked to the sky.

"You wanna go higher?" I asked.

"No," she said very quickly. "This is way higher than five reallys."

I smiled as I thought about what she said. "Yes it is. A babygirl who is good can go five reallys high on a swing. A babygirl who makes it to the top of a ferris wheel must be a very brave girl."I said fondly.

There was a moment of silence between us. "How many reallys is the top of a ferris wheel, Daddy?" she asked inquisitively.

"Hmm," I said thinking. "At least 25."

Then she looked up at the stars in the sky. "And how many reallys would it take to get up there?"she asked.

"A million," I said jokingly.

"So if a babygirl who is good can go five reallys high, and a babygirl who is brave can go 25 reallys high, what kind of a babygirl can go a million really high?" she asked with a big grin on her face.

My smile grew wide and I had to keep from laughing. “Well…” I started trying to think of a one-liner to top hers. “I guess that babygirl had better be……..an astronaut.”

Right at that moment, the ride started up again, and she jumped at the loud noise. She re-buried her face in my chest, and once again gripped off the blood circulation in my arm.

“Princess, we’re getting lower to the ground. You just survived the top of the ferris wheel. This should be a piece of cake for you know.” I said.

“I’m just a babygirl, Daddy,” she said, owning the moment as she always did.

I broke out into hysterical laughter, embraced her, kissed her on the forehead, and said, “You certainly are.”

We got off the ferris wheel, and quite to the opposite of the way she got on, she jumped off and down the stairs we ran.

“Where are we headed now?” I asked.

“The pee-zees,” she said. “I saw where they were up there.”

“The pee-zees?” I asked as she grabbed my hand and led the way.

What she took us to was the flying trapeze rides (the swings with the long chains that spin you around). “Oh! The Pee-Zees!” I exclaimed.

“It’s your favorite ride, right?” she asked.

“Without a doubt,” I grinned. “Followed closely by bumper cars.”

The line for this ride was little longer. So I took her into my arms, and against my chest. We didn’t say much. It was kind of hard to talk the way we wanted to. We were standing in a line, but sometimes words are important and actions speak just as loudly and clearly and with as much affection as a gentle tone.

A flying trapeze can take like 30 people at once. So the lines keep moving. I’m a patient individual, but lines at amusement parks get the best of me. That’s why I like this one so much. And before we knew it, it was our turn.

We found swings right next to one another, simply because we were that incessantly in love. We latched ourselves in. I looked over at her and said, “I think this swing might be a little more exciting than the one in the park.”

I faced back front and got ready for the ride to begin when she said: “I doubt it.”

I looked back at her, made speechless by her kind words once again. Her face was beaming with life. She continued: “The operators of this ride don’t care how it makes you feel.”

Right at that moment, the swings began spinning and in seconds we were flying around in a circle. I looked over at her again.

Her hair was blowing straight back. And she laughed. Oh my. I loved to listen to her laugh. This was a kind of ride that even I could enjoy. I have a really weak stomach. So roller coasters were out. The sight of one of those things rolling by was enough to make me weary.

The ride slowed down, the swings came to a rest, and we got off. We exited the ride, and I came to a stop. I put my hands on my hips, and had a puzzled look on my face.

“Food?” she asked.

“Yeah,” I replied. Sometimes even the flying trapeze ride will get the best of my stomach.

We walked slowly as I tried to get my stomach to settle. She put her arm around my back and rubbed my stomach with her other hand, trying to soothe. Smiling, I thanked her.

We went to the nearest food stand and she ordered for us as I stood there still trying to regain my composure.

"A barbeque sandwich, the biggest order of fries you've got and two cokes," she ordered knowing exactly what I wanted and moreover what my stomach needed at that moment.

We got the food and sat at the first picnic table we found. I began to inhale this barbeque sandwich. She loaded her fries with salt, ketchup, and vinegar. It was one of her passions. She looked over at me, and brushed my hair back out my face with her fingertips. Then at the back of my head, she lightly drew her fingernails across my scalp and through my hair. It felt really good.

I finished eating, and quietly burped. "I feel better. What would you like to do now?" I asked her.

"I'd like to go home," she replied honestly.

I looked at her with an "I'm sorry" look on my face, and was about to apologize when she put her pointer finger over my lips.

"Shh," she whispered softly. "It's time for me to take care of you. I want you to let me do that. There will be another carnival at some point soon, and I know you will give me more memories, all the love you have inside and more. But right now, it's time take care of you."

"As you wish, Love. Thank you," I replied.

We left the carnival arm in arm. On the way back to the car, I looked up at the sky and the stars again?

"What do you see?" she asked.

"I see the dippers getting smaller and Orion getting bigger," I replied.

She smiled. "Tell me about them, Daddy," she said laying her head on my shoulder.

"Well, in the summer you have the big dipper and the little dipper. Constellations. They are the biggest two things in the summer sky. And in the winter, you have Orion as the biggest thing in the sky."

"What about in the fall?" she asked.

"I have no idea," I said, laughing.

We got to the car. I opened the driver's side door, sat down, and she crawled over top of me to the passenger's side. As she was crawling, I placed my hand on her diapered bottom to "check". She sat in the passenger's seat, and looked straight forward with the biggest grin on her face.

"You little angel, you," I said while motioning for her to lie down on the front seat. She did so, and as I unfastened fastened the straps on the "bib" of her overall shorts, I put her pacifier in her mouth and went through the usual routine. First I handed her the teddy bear which she grabbed and hugged for dear life. Next, I handed her the blanket which she grabbed, wrapped her teddy bear in, and hugged for dear life.

I untied her sneakers and took them off her feet and then slid the overall shorts off of her. I looked at her and could tell that she was feeling “little” once more. Obediently, she relaxed her body so I could unfasten her diaper. I raised her legs and bottom up and into the air while removing the wet diaper beneath her. I took my fingertips to her bare bottom and tickled her. She thrashed around trying to free her legs from the tickle “monster”, but settled back down when I lowered her onto a new diaper and fastened her in.

I started up the car and she crawled to the middle of the front seat, placed her head on my shoulder, and we drove home. Along the way, she kept gazing up out the sun roof, and muttering something behind her pacifier that sounded like “orange”. I kept asking her what she was saying. Finally, she pointed to the sky.

“Orion,” I pronounced for her.

We got home, and I bundled up the trash and her diaper bag in one arm, and I carried her in the other arm. We entered our house, I tossed the trash, set the diaper bag down, and took her to the couch. I laid her down, and went back into the kitchen for a moment.

“So what do you want to do tomorrow?” I said, jokingly from the kitchen.

She smiled, and answered without missing a beat. “Keep thinking about today.”

She turned the TV on, and flipped through the stations until she found a movie she wanted to watch. I returned to the living room to hear: “Oh My God! Oh My God, you guys! Oh My God! Oh My God, you guys!” Ah yes, she has chosen to watch Legally Blonde: The Musical……again.

I laid down on the couch. She crawled on top of me, turned her head towards the TV laid down on top of me. I took the pacifier from her mouth and inserted a bottle of milk. She took the nipple in and began to drink. I covered our bodies with a blanket and prepared to watch …….. Legally Blonde: The Musical……again.

Five minutes into the movie, the bottle was empty, and she was asleep. I lightly patted her back, and in her breathing she burped. I closed my eyes as well.

What a day it had been.

The End

Zorro Daddy's Complete ABDL Library

Gabriel and Gina

When Gina revealed a love for a fetish to a friend during a drunken Saturday night college party, she had no idea that she would be living out that fetish with him in a few short days.

On this autumn weekend at a college campus, Gina sees her most erotic wishes come true as she learns how much she enjoys being submissive. Her fantasies become a reality, heating up at the end in a sexual climax that leaves her body and her mind in a state of absolute ecstasy.

This story is a romantic fantasy with heavy sexual content, situations and actions. It is adult material and not intended for anyone under the age of 18.

Rock-a-Bye BabyGirls: *Thoughts and Other Journeys of the Mind*

These are short writings that touch upon the emotions felt by the male and female in an infantilism role playing setting and/or relationship. Topics include, but are not limited to: concepts of feeling little, the attachments to and emotional affects of having and using baby items, security, safety, comfort, helplessness, vulnerability, love, respect, overcoming fears and alibis, exploring one's deepest desire, and one's most well kept secrets.

Every writing builds off the previous one in concept and appeal. Nothing in this section is written in story format. Names and locations are generalized and not defined.

Rock-a-Bye BabyGirls: *Short and Sweet Stories*

These are writings which are written in a loose story format. Some are in a style of a love letter that he wrote to her, thoughts within his mind as he watches her role play, his reflections and remembrances of previous role playing encounters with her, recalled thoughts of her which further strengthens his adoration and love for her, and lists desires, wishes, wants, needs, cravings and pride within his heart and soul.

Names and locations are generalized and not defined.

The Zeke and Lily Stories

Before Zeke (an author) and Lily (a newspaper columnist) met, they were perfect strangers who shared a common interest in a role playing fetish. They were perfect for each other and though they lived in the same city, they may never have met until Lily happened upon Zeke's profile online.

This collection of stories tells their tale, from courting to love to a possible happily ever after.

Zeke and Lily: *Once Upon a Beginning*

The story of the day they first met face-to-face at a mall in Lancaster County, PA.

Zeke and Lily: *Overnight*

Zeke and Lily spend the night in his apartment. The result is an evening of events where their separate lives finally collide and they fall in love. By morning, their fantasies had turned into their reality together. But will it lead to a "happily ever after" for them?

Zeke and Lily: *Making a Memory*

Zeke and Lily have bonded their hearts. Their common interest in infantilism has grown into a love for each other. As they head off on a Bahamas vacation, that love deepens. But trouble is on the horizon.

Lily, still letting go of her troubled past, has a secret she deliberately kept from Zeke. Her fear that he will no longer love her increases and she begins to get sick over the decision to tell him the truth. Zeke has a question to ask Lily. It is a question that is weighing on his heart.

As they enjoy their time in the Caribbean, they both struggle within to overcome their fears. But something happens while in the Bahamas that delays their chance to get the truth out, and they may not recover.

Do Zeke and Lily come home together or did their fantasy love just die in the Bahamas?

www.ingramcontent.com/pod-product-compliance
Ingram Content Group UK Ltd.
Pitfield, Milton Keynes, MK11 3LW, UK
UKHW020238250726
13967UKWH00001B/441